Lily and Bear

Lisa Stubbs

A Paula Wiseman Book
Simon & Schuster Books for Young Readers
New York London Toronto Sydney New Delhi

To my Lily, Skyla, and Sonny for their love and inspiration,
to Jodie for her support and loveliness,
and to David and Leilani for their wonderful energy and enthusiasm

SIMON & SCHUSTER BOOKS FOR YOUNG READERS
An imprint of Simon & Schuster Children's Publishing Division
1230 Avenue of the Americas, New York, New York 10020
Copyright © 2015 by Lisa Stubbs
Originally published in 2015 in Great Britain by Boxer Books Limited
First US edition 2015
SIMON & SCHUSTER BOOKS FOR YOUNG READERS is a trademark of Simon & Schuster, Inc.
For information about special discounts for bulk purchases, please contact Simon & Schuster
Special Sales at 1-866-506-1949 or business@simonandschuster.com.
The Simon & Schuster Speakers Bureau can bring authors to your live event. For more information or to book an event,
contact the Simon & Schuster Speakers Bureau at 1-866-248-3049 or visit our website at www.simonspeakers.com.
Book design by Tom Daly
The text for this book is set in Goudy Old Style.
The illustrations for this book were screen printed using
acrylic and then finished with watercolor and pencil crayon.
Manufactured in China / 0115 BOX
2 4 6 8 10 9 7 5 3 1
Library of Congress Cataloging-in-Publication Data
Stubbs, Lisa, author, illustrator.
Lily and Bear / Lisa Stubbs.
pages cm
"A Paula Wiseman Book."
Summary: Lily loves to draw, but when she draws Bear they quickly become friends,
first doing all of the things that Lily enjoys, and then doing Bear's favorite things.
ISBN 978-1-4814-4416-3 (hardcover) — ISBN 978-1-4814-4417-0 (ebook)
[1. Best friends—Fiction. 2. Friendship—Fiction. 3. Drawing—Fiction. 4. Bears—Fiction.] I. Title.
PZ7.S93755Lil 2015   [E]—dc23   2014035156

Lily loved to draw.
She drew
cats and girls,
birds and boats,
and houses
and hearts.

She drew the sea
and a pirate ship
and a teapot.

She drew tricycles
and a banjo.
And then she drew . . .

Bear.

Lily loved Bear and Bear loved Lily.

Lily took Bear by the paw. . . .

They attended royal tea parties

and sailed carpet seas.

They did Lily's favorite thing
and drew big pictures.

Then they raced
around on tricycles.

But best of all, they sang really loudly, while Bear played the banjo brilliantly.

Lily loved Bear and Bear loved Lily.

After a while, Bear sat down.

He didn't want to attend royal tea parties, sail pirate ships, or ride tricycles anymore. Bear wanted to do Bear things.

Lily loved Bear and Bear loved Lily so Bear took Lily by the hand. . . .

They picked
huckleberries
and ate them
from Bear's paws.

They caught
slippery, jumping
fish in the river.

They did Bear's
favorite thing
and scratched
their backs on
a knotty pine.

Then
they rolled
down the
mountainside.

But best of all, as the stars started to shine, they sang a really quiet song while Bear gently played the banjo brilliantly, until . . .

. . . it was time to
sleep and dream of
their next adventure.

"I love you, Bear."
"And I love you, Lily."